Dear Santa, Please Come to the 19th Floor

YIN • CHRIS SOENTPIET

PUFFIN BOOKS
An Imprint of Penguin Group (USA) Inc.

In a few days, Christmas will arrive. I zigzag around the park with my best friend, Carlos, in his wheelchair. Since kindergarten we've played together and dreamed together. Like two peas in a pod.

Since the accident Carlos isn't the same. My mama said his spinal cord was damaged. When Carlos found out he might never walk again, he got angry. One time he threw his favorite basketball out the window. That basketball was a gift his poppa gave him before he moved away.

"Time to come up," a voice screams from above.

"Oh, oh, that's my mom, let's go," Carlos says. "Charge!" Carlos navigates and I push as we race to our building.

"You have the key?" Carlos asks.

"Nope, thought you had it."

No one is supposed to get into our building without the key. I knock for someone to open the locked lobby door. Mrs. Perez from the thirteenth floor, her hair curlers tight as springs, opens it for us.

"Gracias," thank you, I say in Spanish.

Inside the building, we wait for the elevator. More and more people come and wait. Finally it arrives. Jose, who works as a security guard, holds the elevator door open for all of us.

"Con permiso," excuse me, I say, and we sandwich our way into the crowded elevator.

As Buddy the Wino stumbles his way toward the elevator, Jose covers his nose from Buddy's breath.

"You'd better get to your job on time so you don't get fired again," Jose whispers to him.

The door slides open on the second floor and Buddy almost trips off the elevator.

"Threee. . . . Fooour. . . . Fiiiiiiive," we count.

"Getting off," old man Simms says.

"Teeeeeen. . . . Eeeeleeeeeeven. . . . Tweeeelve. . . . Thirteen." Mrs. Perez, clutching her bag full of groceries from the local bodega, shuffles out.

"Fiffffteeen. . . . Ssssixteeen. . . . Seeeeveeeenteen."

"Eeeeeighteen."

Jose's stop. "You boys be good." He smiles and steps off.

We're the last to get off since Carlos lives on the nineteenth floor, all the way at the top.

"And nineteeeeeen!" Carlos and I slip through the quick-closing elevator doors and race down the hallway to his apartment at 19G.

Carlos' mama gives him a nice welcome hug. Then she turns to me and gives me a hug. My mama is always working at the hospital, so Mrs. G. is like an aunt to me.

At the dinner table, Mrs. G. piles our plates with lots of spaghetti and meat sauce.

"Hey, Christmas is near. What would you like Santa to bring?" Mrs. G. asks.

"Santa never comes here to this neighborhood," I reply.

Rachel, Carlos' sister, says, "We don't even have a fireplace or chimney."

"He would never come anyway. Santa wouldn't want to see me in a wheelchair," Carlos says sadly.

There is silence in the room. I can see tears start to well in Mrs. G.'s eyes.

"Well, we have to understand that Santa Claus is a very busy man," she explains. "He probably doesn't know you boys live up here."

Rachel thinks hard. "Even if he knew, he couldn't get past the lobby. He doesn't have the key. Then he'd have to take the elevator all the way up. Too much trouble for an important guy like him. Unless . . ."

"Unless what?" I mumble between mouthfuls of spaghetti.

"We could write him a letter with instructions on how to get in," Rachel says.

"That's silly," Carlos says. But I look at Rachel and I have an idea.

After dinner, Carlos is frustrated that he has to do his therapy exercises with Mrs. G. I sneak to the computer in the other room. It's used, Social Services gave it to Carlos and his family, but it works. Rachel sneaks in too.

"Try santaclaus@northpole.com," she whispers. I start to type.

```
Dear Santa,
Please come to the 19th floor.
When you arrive at my building,
ring the intercom #11A. I can
buzz you through the locked
doors. Then I can take you up to
Carlos' apartment. My pal Carlos
is in a wheelchair now and could
use a good surprise.
             Your buddy, Willy
P.S. Carlos' sister said to
leave your reindeer on the street
with the other parked cars or else
you'll get a ticket.
```

With the mouse, I click on the SEND button. I hope Santa comes. That will make Carlos' Christmas.

Before the accident, Carlos and I would stare out the windows of the nineteenth floor at the stars and dream together. He'd say, "I'm going to be a basketball player—I'm already good at defense."

"I want to be...an astronomer," I'd say.

We don't dream like we used to. Now I stare out the window at the stars alone.

"It's getting late, Willy!" Mrs. G. calls out. I head back to my apartment on the eleventh floor and pass some real tough-looking kids that hang out. Our entire neighborhood is scary and rough. Why would Santa want to come here!

Days pass, and soon it is Christmas Eve day. Carlos stays home with his family, and I stay at home with Mama.

"Willy, it's almost eleven o'clock. Aren't you going to bed?" Mama asks.

"But tonight Santa will come," I say.

"You have to be asleep for him to come." Mama tucks me into bed. "Sweet dreams, baby," she softly coos.

In bed, I toss and turn. Santa has to come for Carlos. I get up and look out my window. No Santa in sight.

I lie down on my bed and minutes pass. I look out my window again, further down the street. I see someone in a red suit walking toward my building.

It's him!

I grab my jacket and quietly sneak out of my apartment. I head to the elevators on our floor. I wait and wait but neither elevator comes. So I skip down the steps as fast as lightning.

I hold my breath and stand perfectly still as he stares at the intercom. He looks exactly like what I imagined.

But he's confused. He doesn't know which button to press, and he can't get through the front doors. I open the door for him. "Santa, is that you?"

"HO . . . HO . . . HO," he cheers. "Special stop for the nineteenth floor!"

"I'm Willy."

"Just who I want. I think your intercom is broken," Santa says.

I grab Santa by the wrist and pull him through the door. "Don't worry, you're in."

Santa and I wait for the elevator to take us up. Minutes pass and it does not come. I notice Santa looking at his watch. More minutes pass and still no elevators. Santa looks at his watch again. I can tell Santa can't wait much longer. I have an idea.

I take Santa by the arm and yank him toward the building's stairs.

Santa stares up at the dark staircase. His nose twitches at the air. It smells like dirty socks. But Santa isn't a man to disappoint, so he takes off his hat.

"To the nineteenth floor we go!" he shouts.

He leaves his hat behind.

We make our way to the second floor, where Buddy the Wino is hanging out on the steps.

"He doesn't have a job," I whisper to Santa. "Can't show up for work on time. He gets fired all the time."

Santa takes off his watch. "Merry Christmas, my friend," he cheers. "This will help you get places on time."

"Hey, thanks!" Buddy smiles with delight.

We climb to the third floor, the fourth. "My feet are killing me," Santa says. He takes off his boots. He pulls a pair of sneakers out of his bag. "These are just my size." Santa struggles to get his feet snugly into the new sneakers.

He leaves his heavy boots behind.

We make our way to the fifth floor, the sixth. At the seventh, Manny is mopping the stairs, bored as ever. "Watch it," he grumps. "The floor is slippery."

"Ho, ho, ho. Why are you working? It's Christmas Eve!" Santa asks.

Manny answers with a deep sigh. "Overtime."

Santa hands Manny a gift. "Maybe this will make your overtime more exciting."

Manny opens the gift, and admires a brand-new radio. "Thanks!" Manny tunes to his favorite channel and mops the floor to the beat of the music.

We continue up to the eighth floor, ninth. At the tenth floor, Santa sits down. "I haven't eaten since breakfast," he huffs.

I dig in my pockets. Just Santa's luck, I find some wrapped cookies that we get free at school. "Have one."

"How did you know I like cookies?" He giggles and munches on the cookie. He takes another deep breath and marches up to the eleventh floor. And the twelfth.

Meanwhile, on the thirteenth floor, Mrs. Perez, her curlers still in, is trying to get her cat out of the fire hose box. Santa reaches into his bag. He gives Mrs. Perez a hair dryer, and the cat a box of catnip. "A gift indeed is a gift in need," he says, and he pants up the stairs.

We make our way up to the fourteenth floor. Santa huffs and puffs. Sweat is streaming from Santa's forehead. "Wait, Willy."

Santa leaves his belt, his white gloves and his heavy red coat behind.

"We're almost there," I shout. "Just a few flights more. Any minute now!" But when we arrive at the fifteenth floor, the light is out.

"Never fear, light is near!" Santa gasps for more breath. He fumbles in his bag for a lightbulb. "Aha, found one!"

"Santa, give me a boost," I say. Santa inhales and exhales deeply and tries to lift me up. I turn the lightbulb into the socket. The red glow makes it look even more like Christmas.

Now Santa is practically crawling on his knees up to the sixteenth floor, then the seventeenth.

On the eighteenth floor, Santa is worn out and collapses. "I can't go any farther," he wheezes.

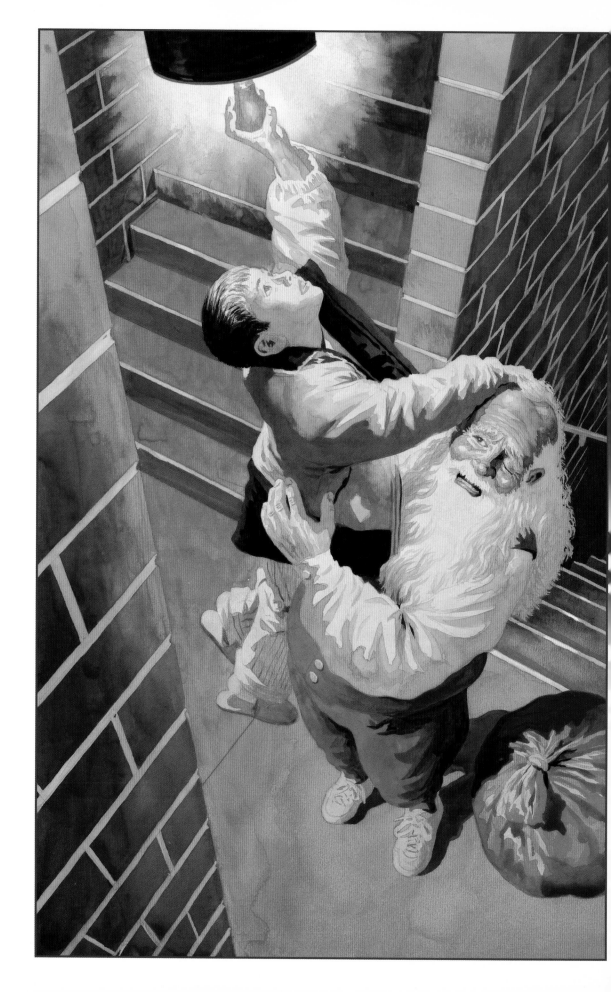

Suddenly Jose comes up from behind—wearing Santa's hat, gloves, boots and suit! "Guess what I found going up the stairs." He spins himself in a circle like a fashion model.

"Hey, Willy, who's the old guy on the floor?" Jose points to Santa.

"That's Santa Claus," I try to explain, "and you're wearing his clothes."

"No way," Jose snaps. "We don't have fireplaces or chimneys."

"He's here to see Carlos," I reply to Jose. "But I'm not sure he can climb one step more."

Santa lays a finger aside of his nose and gestures for Jose to go up the last flight of stairs.

And what do you know, Jose takes Santa's bag. "I'll finish the job for you, Santa!"

Top of the stairs, I shout, "We'll be back for you, Santa!"

We race to Carlos' door and I turn the doorknob. It's locked.

But suddenly the door creeps open. "Hey, I could hear you all the way from the East River. What's going on?" Carlos rubs his droopy eyes.

"It's Santa," I holler. "He's really here on the nineteenth floor!"

"Ho . . . ho . . . ho?" Jose belts out a weak cheer. "Merry Christmas!"

"Santa Claus, phooey. That's Jose," Carlos snaps in disappointment. "I knew Santa would never come."

Suddenly, from behind me, a strong voice calls out.

"HO . . . HO . . . HO . . . MERRY CHRISTMAS!"

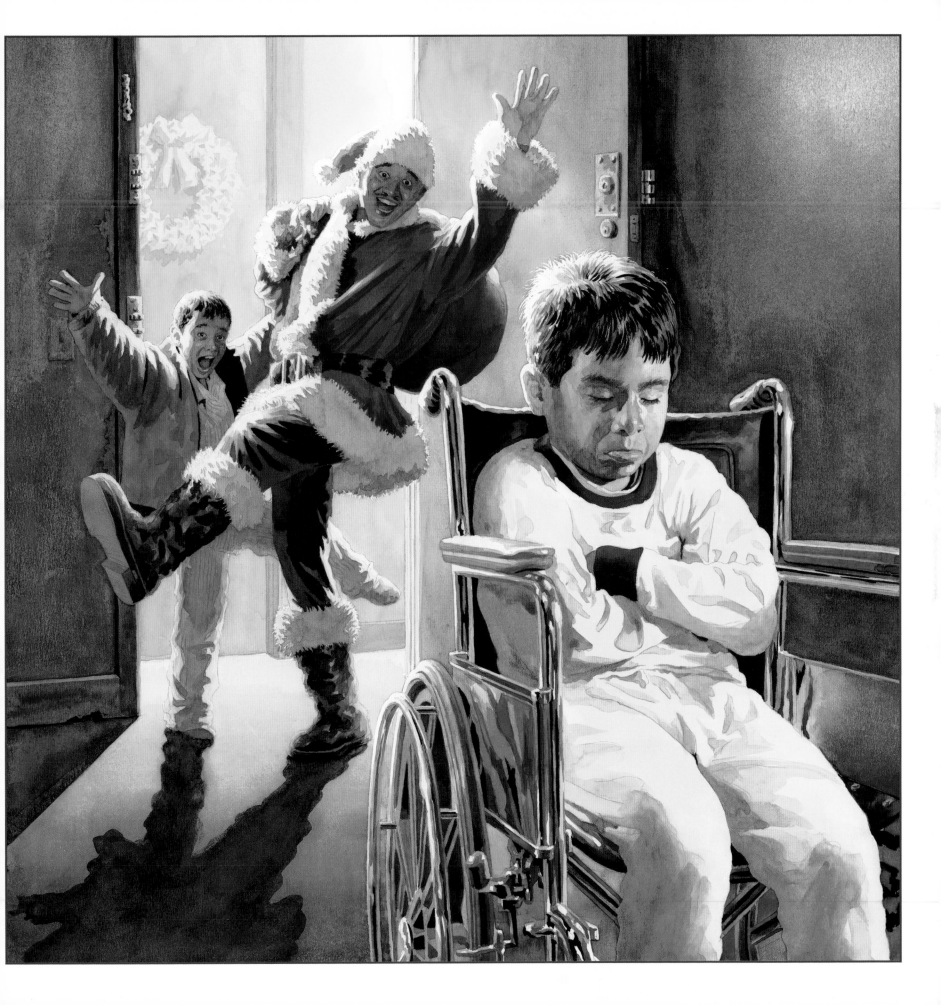

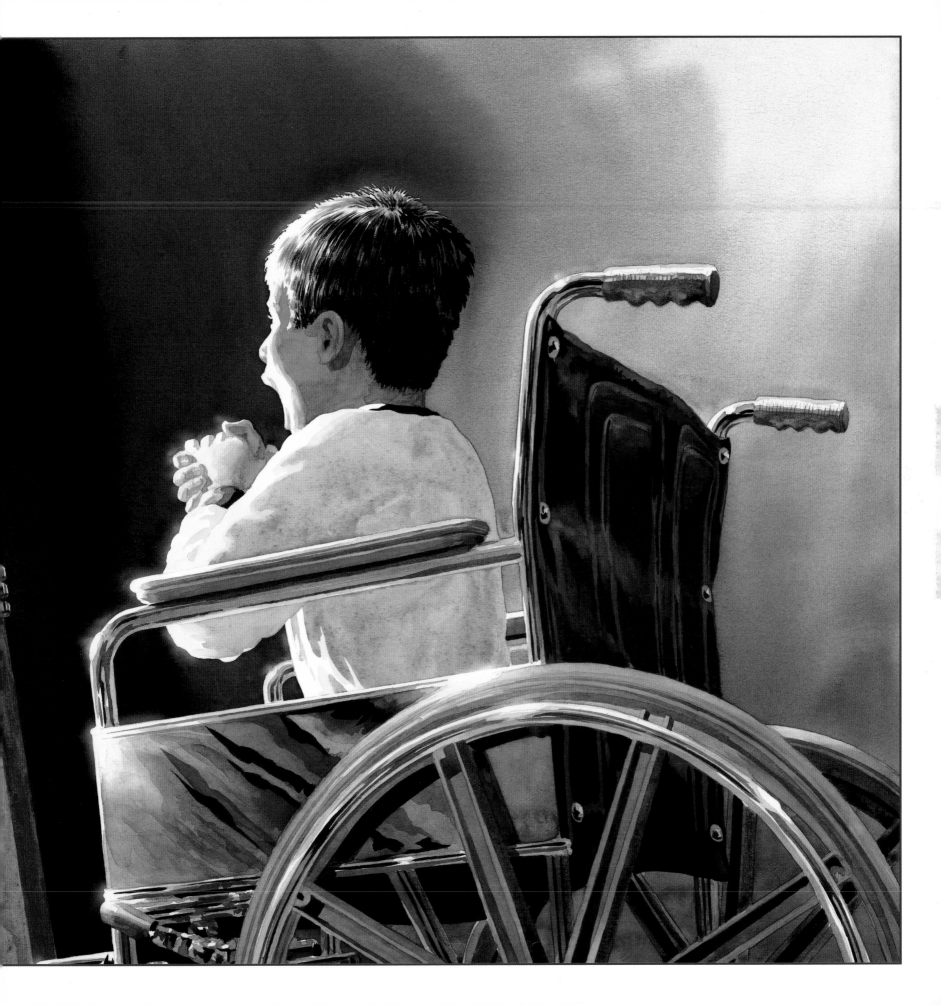

Santa hands Carlos a gift. He tears the gift open and, surprise, finds—"A basketball?"

Carlos' face falls flat. "In case you haven't noticed, Santa, I'm in a wheelchair," he mocks.

"So?" Santa says. "And I'll bet you're still good at defense."

There is silence in the room. But for the first time, Carlos doesn't say no.

Next thing, Santa hands a present to ME!

"I got two e-mails," he says. "One from Willy. And one—from Carlos." Santa pulls a letter from his pocket.

Santa clears his throat and reads,

```
Dear Santa,
Ever since my accident, my
best buddy Willy isn't the same.
It makes me sad. We live in a
rough neighborhood—79 Columbus
Street—and you may not want to
come. But if you do, it will
really cheer Willy up.
                    From, Carlos
```

Santa motions me to open the box and winks to Carlos. I tear the gift wrap off and discover a telescope! I give Carlos a high five.

Santa is already changing back into his uniform, and he drops off a gift for Rachel as well.

Santa leaves Carlos' apartment not through a fireplace or chimney but through the front door. His "HO . . . HO . . . HO . . . MERRY CHRISTMAS!" echoes through the hallway.

I wish he could have stayed, but that's okay. "He has lots of other kids to visit," Mama says. "Maybe they need hope too."

"Maybe so," I say, because that was the real gift he'd given both Carlos and me, hope.

PUFFIN BOOKS
Published by the Penguin Group
Penguin Young Readers Group, 345 Hudson Street, New York, New York 10014, U.S.A.
Penguin Group (Canada), 90 Eglinton Avenue East, Suite 700, Toronto, Ontario, Canada M4P 2Y3 (a division of Pearson Penguin Canada Inc.)
Penguin Books Ltd, 80 Strand, London WC2R 0RL, England
Penguin Ireland, 25 St Stephen's Green, Dublin 2, Ireland (a division of Penguin Books Ltd)
Penguin Group (Australia), 250 Camberwell Road, Camberwell, Victoria 3124, Australia (a division of Pearson Australia Group Pty Ltd)
Penguin Books India Pvt Ltd, 11 Community Centre, Panchsheel Park, New Delhi - 110 017, India
Penguin Group (NZ), 67 Apollo Drive, Rosedale, Auckland 0632, New Zealand (a division of Pearson New Zealand Ltd.)
Penguin Books (South Africa) (Pty) Ltd, 24 Sturdee Avenue, Rosebank, Johannesburg 2196, South Africa

Registered Offices: Penguin Books Ltd, 80 Strand, London WC2R 0RL, England

First published in the United States of America by Philomel Books, a division of Penguin Putnam Books for Young Readers, 2002
Published by Puffin Books, a division of Penguin Young Readers Group, 2011

1 3 5 7 9 10 8 6 4 2

Patricia Lee Gauch, Editor
Text copyright © 2002 by Yin. Illustrations copyright © 2002 by Chris Soentpiet. All rights reserved.

LIBRARY OF CONGRESS CATALOGING-IN-PUBLICATION DATA IS AVAILABLE.

Puffin Books ISBN 978–0–14–241931–1

Manufactured in China
Book design by Semadar Megged. The text is set in 14-point Golden Cockerel.
The illustrations are rendered in watercolors on watercolor paper.